75th
ANNIVERSARY
The WIZARD of OZ

The WIZARD of OZ ™

ADAPTED BY BETH BRACKEN

Based on the screenplay by Noel Langley, Florence Ryerson,
and Edgar Allan Woolf
From the book by L. Frank Baum

Capstone Young Readers

DOROTHY GALE

lived on a farm in Kansas, but she dreamed of a place that was over the rainbow . . .

SHE WASN'T IN KANSAS ANYMORE . . . .

"TOTO, I THINK WE MUST BE OVER THE RAINBOW!" she said.

Wherever she was, it was a magical and mysterious place.

The wild twister had brought Dorothy and her dog, Toto, to the Land of Oz.

And it was here that she met Glinda the Good Witch of the North, who sailed down on a pink bubble to greet her.

Glinda asked Dorothy, "Are you a good witch or a bad witch?"

"Who, me?" Dorothy answered. "I'm not a witch at all."

You see, when Dorothy's house landed in Munchkinland, it fell on the Wicked Witch of the East—leaving only her Ruby Slippers.

The Witch was dead and the Munchkins were free. That made the Munchkins very happy.

But there was another bad witch, the Wicked Witch of the West. And she was very, very mad. She quickly appeared to claim the Ruby Slippers.

But it was too late. With the touch of her magic wand, Glinda moved the glittering shoes to Dorothy's feet.

Before the Wicked Witch left, she told Dorothy,

"I'LL GET YOU, MY PRETTY, AND YOUR LITTLE DOG TOO!"

The Witch was scary, and all Dorothy wanted to do was go home to Auntie Em and Uncle Henry and everyone else she knew and loved.

But no one knew how to get her home . . . except one person.

THE GREAT AND POWERFUL WIZARD OF OZ.

And to find him, Dorothy had to follow the Yellow Brick Road.

SHE WAS OFF
TO SEE THE
WONDERFUL
WIZARD OF OZ.

When Dorothy came to a fork in the road, she didn't know where to go. The Scarecrow didn't, either.

After all, he didn't have a brain. Maybe the Wizard of
Oz could give him one.

Soon, the Scarecrow was off to the Emerald City with Dorothy,
both of them following the Yellow Brick Road.

n an apple orchard, Dorothy and the Scarecrow came across a man made of tin. All he needed was a bit of oil to help him talk and walk again.

But the poor Tin Man didn't have a heart.

And so he, too, decided to travel to see the Great and Powerful Wizard of Oz.

Now there were three of them, plus Toto, off to see the Wizard.

But before they could get to the Wizard of Oz, they had to travel through a creepy forest.

A FOREST FULL OF TIGERS, BEARS, AND . . .

. . . LIONS.

All of a sudden, a lion leaped onto the road. "GRRR!" he roared.

But this Lion wasn't mean. In fact, he was a great big coward.

He didn't have any courage.

But maybe the Wizard of Oz could give him some too.

Now there were four friends heading to the Emerald City.

eanwhile, not far away, the Wicked Witch was watching the foursome in her crystal ball. She didn't want Dorothy and her friends to reach the Emerald City.

The Wicked Witch sent them into a field of poppies, which made them very sleepy.

But the Good Witch of the North was watching, too.

She waved her wand and sent snow to the field of poppies . . .
just in time to wake Dorothy up.

It was a good thing, because they were almost to . . .

...THE EMERALD CITY.

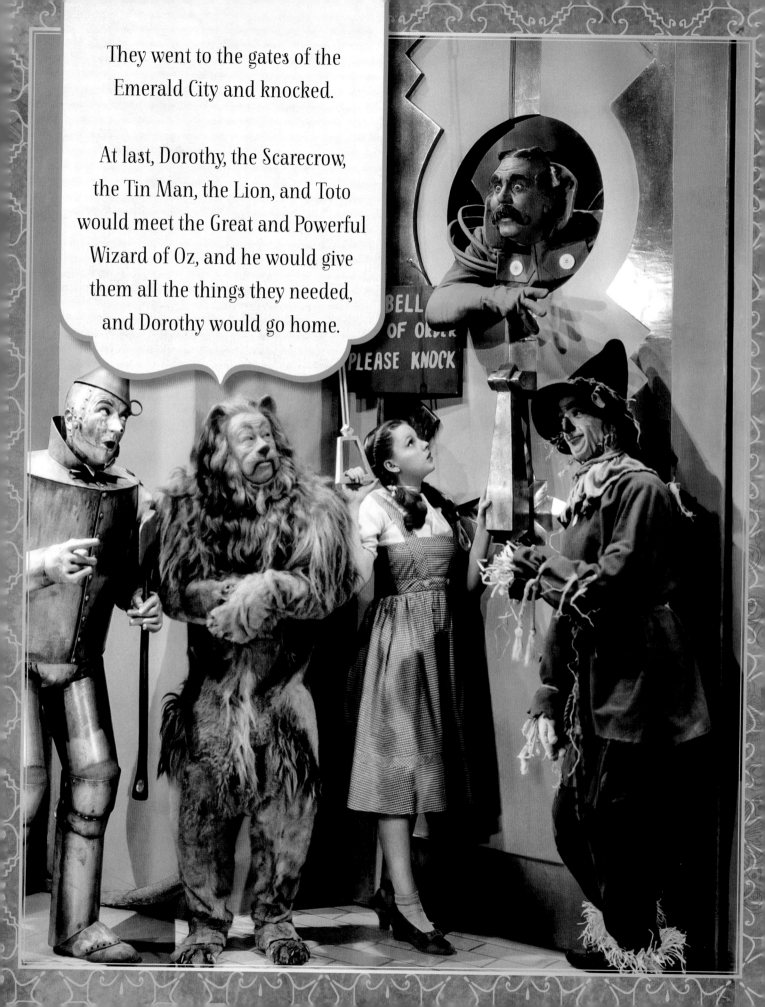

They went to the gates of the
Emerald City and knocked.

At last, Dorothy, the Scarecrow,
the Tin Man, the Lion, and Toto
would meet the Great and Powerful
Wizard of Oz, and he would give
them all the things they needed,
and Dorothy would go home.

Except it wasn't that easy. The Wizard said he'd grant their wishes . . .

. . . but first, they had to perform a very small task.

They had to bring back the Wicked Witch's broomstick.

 o find the Witch's castle, they had to travel through the Haunted Forest.

Getting the broomstick was not easy. The Wicked Witch of the West was cruel and mean.

When the Witch tried to set the Scarecrow on fire, Dorothy threw water on the Scarecrow to put out the flames.

But the water splashed in the Witch's face . . . and she melted.

Soon nothing was left but her cloak, hat, and broom.

Back in the Emerald City, the Wizard of Oz granted all of their wishes.

THE SCARECROW GOT A BRAIN.

THE TIN MAN GOT A HEART.

THE LION GOT COURAGE.

And Dorothy used the magic of her Ruby Slippers, clicked
her heels three times, and repeated . . .

"THERE'S
NO PLACE
LIKE HOME."

THE END

Published in 2013 by Capstone Young Readers
A Capstone Imprint
1710 Roe Crest Drive
North Mankato, Minnesota 56003
www.capstoneyoungreaders.com

Library of Congress Cataloging-in-Publication Data
Bracken, Beth.
The Wizard of Oz / by Beth Bracken.
p. cm.
Summary: Dorothy is transported over the rainbow in this picture book adaptation of the classic movie, The Wizard of Oz.
ISBN 978-1-62370-026-3
1. Baum, L. Frank (Lyman Frank), 1856-1919. Wizard of Oz.--Adaptations. 2. Oz (Imaginary place)--Juvenile fiction. 3. Gale, Dorothy
(Fictitious character)--Juvenile fiction. [1. Baum, L. Frank (Lyman Frank), 1856-1919. Wizard of Oz--Adaptations. 2. Oz (Imaginary
place)--Fiction. 3. Fantasy.] I. Wizard of Oz (Motion picture: 1939) II. Title.
PZ7.B6989Wk 2013
813.6--dc23
2013009504

Image Credits: Shutterstock; Cover/Cloud: Karon Dubke (Capstone)
Art Director: Heather Kindseth Wutschke
Graphic Designer: Heather Kindseth Wutschke and Kristi Carlson

Printed in the United States of America in Stevens Point, Wisconsin.
052013   007389WZF13